Summer
the Holiday
Fairy

For Olivia Cowle

Special thanks to
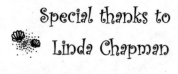
Linda Chapman

ORCHARD BOOKS
338 Euston Road, London NW1 3BH
Orchard Books Australia
Hachette Children's Books
Level 17/207 Kent Street, Sydney, NSW 2000
A Paperback Original
First published in Great Britain in 2005
Text © Working Partners Limited 2005
Rainbow Magic is a registered trademark of Working Partners Limited.
Series created by Working Partners Limited, London W6 0QT
Illustrations © Georgie Ripper 2005
The right of Georgie Ripper to be identified as the illustrator
of this work has been asserted by her in accordance
with the Copyright, Designs and Patents Act, 1988.
A CIP catalogue record for this book is available
from the British Library.
ISBN 1 84362 960 7
9 10
Printed in Great Britain

Summer
the Holiday
Fairy

by Daisy Meadows

illustrated by Georgie Ripper

ORCHARD BOOKS

www.rainbowmagic.co.uk

The Fairyland Palace

Maze

Forest

Orchard

Meadow

Tower

Donkey Rides

Beach

Rockpools

Rainspell Island

Shells

The Curly
Twirly Shell

Come wind, come breeze,
come howling gale,
Whip up waves and billow sail!
Gather up the shells and sand
From every corner of this land.

And with my cunning breezy spells
I'll steal the magic Rainspell Shells.
Then beaches, ice cream, summer fun
Will be spoiled for everyone!

Contents

The Fairy Footprint   11

A Sudden Storm   21

Where Has All the Sand Gone?   37

Jack Frost's Palace   47

The Magic Shell   59

The Fairy Footprint

"Have you finished packing yet, Rachel?" Mrs Walker called up the stairs. "Kirsty and her parents will be here soon."

"Almost finished!" Rachel Walker shouted back. It was the start of the summer holidays and in just a few hours she and her parents would be back on Rainspell Island! Even better,

Kirsty Tate, Rachel's best friend, was
going to be staying there with her parents
too. The two girls had met on that very
island the summer before. It had been a
magical time.

Very magical, Rachel thought with
a smile. She and Kirsty shared an amazing
secret. They were friends with the fairies!
They had first met the fairies when the
king and queen of Fairyland asked
for their help to rescue the Rainbow
Fairies. Since then, Rachel and Kirsty had
had many more adventures with them.

I wonder if we'll see any fairies this
holiday, Rachel thought. She touched the
golden locket she always wore around her
neck. Kirsty had one just the same. They
had been a gift from the Fairy Queen
and they were filled with fairy dust.

Rachel had just two more things left to pack – her washbag and her favourite T-shirt. She hunted through her drawers. Where was it? She glimpsed the corner of a sleeve sticking out from under her bed.

"Oh no!" she groaned. There was a large stain of tomato ketchup on the front.

Feeling cross that she hadn't asked her mum to wash it, she went to the bathroom to get her washbag.

When she came back, she stopped with a gasp. The T-shirt was neatly  folded on the bed and the stain had nearly vanished! There was just one little mark on the sleeve. Rachel bent closer. It wasn't a mark. It was... it was...

It was a tiny, sandy footprint!

A ray of sunshine shone in through the window and the sleeve of her T-shirt glowed.

"Fairy dust!" Rachel breathed.

A car beeped outside.

"Hurry up, Rachel!" Rachel heard her mum's footsteps on the stairs. "Kirsty's here."

Putting her T-shirt in her case, Rachel hurried downstairs.

"Hi, Rachel!" Kirsty cried, running through the front door. Her dark hair was in bunches and she was wearing shorts and a pink t-shirt.

"Sorry, we're a little late!" Mrs Tate, Kirsty's mum, exclaimed. "The car had a flat tyre when we got up this morning."

"Or at least I thought it had," Mr Tate said. "But by the time I'd fetched my tools, the tyre wasn't flat any more. Very strange. " He laughed. "Almost like magic."

Rachel and Kirsty exchanged looks. Magic!

Rachel wanted to tell Kirsty about the fairy footprint but she couldn't say anything in front of their parents. "Um, Kirsty, do you want to come and see my new duvet cover before we go?"

"Sure," Kirsty replied.

They ran upstairs.

Kirsty seemed to realise the duvet cover had just been an excuse. She glanced quickly at the cover, which had a pattern of hearts and stars. "It's lovely," she said before turning to Rachel, her eyes shining.

"So, do you think my dad's tyre was fixed by magic? It was really weird. I was with Dad when he went back with his tools and I'm sure I heard some music – very faint, but it was like the tinkle of an ice cream van."

Rachel couldn't hold her news in any longer. "I bet it was magic!" she said. "A fairy's been here too."

"Really?" Kirsty gasped.

Rachel nodded and told Kirsty about her T-shirt. "There was a tiny sandy footprint on it," she said. "It must have been made by a fairy."

"Let's have a look around!" Kirsty exclaimed. "Maybe the fairy's still here!"

A Sudden Storm

Rachel and Kirsty had just started
looking when Mr Walker opened the
door. "Come on, you two. If we don't
get a move on we'll miss the ferry."

Shooting one last look around
Rachel's bedroom they went downstairs.

They travelled in Rachel's dad's
car on the way to the ferry.

They couldn't discuss fairies with Mr and Mrs Walker sitting in the front but it was fun just to be together again and talk.

"I can't wait to get to Rainspell Island," Rachel declared.

"Me neither," agreed Kirsty. "I want some of Rosie's Rainspell ice cream."

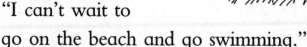

"Oh yes!" Rachel sighed happily. Rosie sold delicious ice cream from her van near the harbour. "I can't wait to go on the beach and go swimming."

"And paddle in the rockpools," Kirsty said.

They grinned at each other. Their holiday was going to be so much fun!

As they got on to the ferry, Mr Tate looked at the blue sky. "It should be a very calm crossing," he commented.

"Good," said Mrs Walker. "I don't want to feel sea-sick!"

As the ferry chugged across the flat green sea, Rachel and Kirsty watched eagerly for the first glimpse of Rainspell Island.

"There it is!" Kirsty exclaimed as a rocky island appeared on the horizon. Suddenly she shivered. "Brrr. The sun's gone in!"

The girls looked up. Big black clouds were racing across the sky.

"The sea's getting rougher," Rachel said.

"Goodness, what a difference in the weather!" Mr Tate exclaimed.

"Do you think it's magic?" Rachel whispered to Kirsty.

"Maybe it's something to do with Jack Frost," Kirsty whispered back. The ferry lurched and she grabbed at her seat.

"I don't feel very well," Mrs Walker said, looking very green. "I think I'd better go in. Are you coming, girls?"

"No, we'll stay out here," Rachel said. The waves were really choppy now and the wind was freezing but she wanted to talk to Kirsty.

"OK, but if it gets any rougher you must come inside," replied Mrs Walker.

"It's got to be magic!" Kirsty said to Rachel as soon as the adults had gone.

"I bet Jack Frost is up to something," Rachel replied.

The waves grew even rougher.

"I think we should go inside," said Kirsty, looking worried.

Rachel nodded. Grabbing on to nearby seats, they staggered towards the door. Suddenly a big wave tossed the boat upwards. Kirsty stumbled and fell. She rolled along the deck and bumped into a pile of ropes. Fighting to keep her balance, Rachel hurried after her. "Are you OK?"

Kirsty nodded. "Yes, thanks."

As she started to get up, Rachel grabbed her arm. "What's that?"

"What?" Kirsty asked.

"That noise," said Rachel. "Listen!"

They both listened. A tiny groaning sound was coming from nearby. And one of the coils of rope looked a bit glittery, even though the sun wasn't shining.

"It's coming from over here!" Kirsty
said. "It's…" She broke off with a gasp.
"Oh!"

There was a fairy lying under the
rope! She had tousled shoulder-length,
honey-blonde hair and
she was wearing a
bright pink top.
A matching
sarong was tied
around her waist
and she had a
necklace made
out of tiny white
shells. Her skin was
pale under her freckles
and she was groaning
and clutching her tummy.

"Hello," Rachel said.

The fairy jumped. For a moment she
looked scared but then she smiled.
"Oh hello, you're Rachel and Kirsty,
aren't you?"

"Yes!" Rachel replied. She felt a thrill
of excitement that the fairy knew who
they were.

"I'm Summer the Holiday Fairy,"
the fairy told them. "I make sure that
summer holidays are special. I…"
She broke off with a moan.

"Are you OK?" Kirsty asked.

"No, I feel sea-sick!" said Summer.
"It's all Jack Frost's fault. He's made
the sea turn rough."

Kirsty looked at Rachel. "We thought
it was Jack Frost!"

"He's been up to all sorts of bad things
on Rainspell Island," Summer said weakly.

Rachel frowned. "What's he been doing?"

Summer moaned again. "I'm sorry. I can't tell you at the moment. I feel too sick! If I didn't feel so bad, I could use my magic seaweed to calm the waves."

"Can we help?" said Kirsty.

Summer nodded and opened her fairy-sized beach bag, embroidered with tiny shells. She took out a strand of seaweed that glittered with green sparkles. "Stroke this over the top of the waves, and the sea will calm down."

Rachel and Kirsty hurried to the side of the ferry. Rachel leant over the rail but the waves looked a long way down.

"It's not going to reach," Rachel said in dismay, dangling the piece of seaweed from her hand. Then she gasped. "Kirsty, look!"

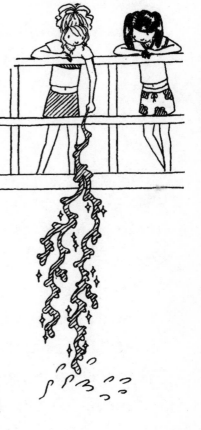

The sparkly seaweed was growing!

"Wow!" Kirsty exclaimed.

The seaweed stretched down and down until it touched the top of the waves.

With a whoosh, a burst of green and
gold sparks fizzed across the water.
Almost immediately the waves began
to calm.

"It's working!" Kirsty cried.

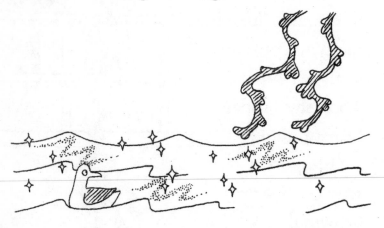

They ran back to Summer. The little
fairy was smoothing down her wavy
hair. "Thank you so much," she said.
"I'm feeling better already!" She grinned
at them. "Did you notice I'd been at
your houses today?"

"You cleaned
my T-shirt!"
Rachel said.

"And mended
my dad's tyre!"
Kirsty added.

Summer nodded.

"I was trying to
make sure Jack Frost
didn't stop you getting
to Rainspell on time. I really need your
help. The goblins have been wrecking
everyone's holidays because Jack Frost
wants Rainspell all for himself."

Her wand made a tinkling sound,
like the faint echo of an ice cream van.

Kirsty nudged Rachel. "That's the
noise I heard when my dad's tyre
was mended."

"Oh, goodness!" Summer exclaimed, looking at her wand. "There must be a new problem on the island. I'll tell you about Jack Frost later. Thanks for helping me!"

She flew into the air in a burst of golden dust. The next second, she was gone.

Rachel beamed at Kirsty. "It looks like we're going to be having a fairy adventure after all!"

Where Has All the Sand Gone?

When the ferry arrived at Rainspell Island, the sky was blue again and the waves lapped gently in the harbour. Rachel skipped with excitement. Even if Jack Frost was making trouble, it was still wonderful to be back on Rainspell.

Kirsty was feeling the same. "This is going to be the best holiday ever!" she declared.

But they soon noticed that something was wrong. Usually everyone on Rainspell Island looked happy, but now there were lots of people going around with glum faces. Even the seagulls were sitting gloomily on the harbour wall instead of swooping joyfully through the sky.

"I wonder why everyone looks so miserable," said Mrs Walker.

When they reached the beach they found out.

There was no sand! Instead of blue sea lapping against the soft golden beach, there were just dull grey pebbles and sharp rocks.

"What's happened?" exclaimed Mrs Tate.

"All the sand just disappeared," said a man passing by. "A storm blew up and when it was over, the sand was gone."

Kirsty and Rachel exchanged horrified looks. Was this Jack Frost's work?

"Oh dear," Mrs Walker said. "I guess you won't be building any sandcastles then, girls."

"Never mind," said Mr Tate, trying to be cheerful. "It's not the end of the world. I'm sure everything else on the island will still be perfect. Let's go and get an ice cream."

But when they reached the ice cream van, they saw a big sign on it that said "CLOSED".

A woman with curly red hair was locking the van. "Rosie!" Kirsty called, recognising the ice-cream seller from the summer before.

She and Rachel ran over. "Are you about to open the van?" Rachel asked.

Rosie shook her head. "I haven't got any ice cream," she said. "It melts as soon as I make it. A few people tried drinking it like soup but it tasted horrible – all salty like sea-water." She sighed. "I don't know what's wrong but nothing I've tried has made a difference."

"Oh, goodness!" Mrs Walker exclaimed. "No sand, no ice cream. This isn't going to be much of a holiday."

Rachel and Kirsty looked at each other in dismay.

"We'll be fine," said Rachel's dad, seeing their faces.

He pointed to a notice pinned to a nearby lamppost. "Look, there's a sailing regatta on in a few days. That should be fun!"

"I suppose so," Mrs Walker agreed, cheering up.

But Rachel and Kirsty weren't so sure. If Jack Frost was really determined to spoil everyone's holiday, who knew what he'd get up to next?

As soon as the unpacking was done, Rachel and Kirsty went for a walk on the beach. It was quiet and lonely without any people sunbathing or playing games.

Kirsty looked for a flat stone to skim across the sea. As she picked it up, a shower of golden dust flew into the air.

"Oh!" Kirsty and Rachel gasped as Summer twirled into the sky.

"Hi there!" called the fairy. "I was just helping a hermit crab. The shell on his back got whisked away by Jack Frost's magic and he didn't have anywhere to live. Look!"

A sad-looking hermit crab was shuffling sideways towards a little hut built out of twigs.

"I built him a
house," Summer
explained. "But I think
he'd rather have his shell back."

"Has Jack Frost taken all the shells?"
Kirsty asked.

Summer nodded.

"Why?" Rachel said.

"I'll show you." Summer raised her
golden wand and a cloud of glittering
fairy dust and tiny shells swirled down.
It smelled of sun tan oil and ice cream.
As it landed on Rachel and Kirsty,
they felt themselves shrinking.

"We're fairies again!" they cried
in delight.

Jack Frost's Palace

Kirsty and Rachel soared up into
the sky with Summer. Fairy dust
glinted in the air behind them.

"Come this way," Summer said.

Rachel and Kirsty followed her
as she swooped over the forest to the
other side of the island. "There's the
maze!" Rachel exclaimed as they flew

over some green hedges laid out in a
twisty pattern.

"And the ruined tower!" Kirsty pointed
to a crumbling stack of yellow stone.

"Almost there!" Summer called.

At a place where the forest met the
beach, she plunged down and
hovered on the spot.

Rachel and Kirsty stared. Half-hidden at the edge of the trees was the most enormous sandcastle they had ever seen. It was decorated with thousands and thousands of shells. A large sea-water moat had been built around it, patrolled by four ugly goblins with long noses and big feet.

"So that's where all the sand and shells have gone!" Kirsty said, looking at the castle's shell-studded walls.

"Yes," replied Summer. "Jack Frost went to the sandcastle competition last week and cast a spell to turn the winning castle into a palace for his summer holidays. It was so big he needed all the sand from the beach and all the shells." She shook her head. "Worst of all, he stole the three special Rainspell Shells from their cave under the sea."

"What are the Rainspell Shells?" Rachel asked curiously.

"They're magic shells that make Rainspell Island the best place ever for a holiday,' Summer explained. "The first is a tall, pink-and-cream spiral shell. It makes all the holiday food on Rainspell, like Rosie's ice cream, taste extra delicious. The second is a beautiful conch shell that controls the wind and waves, making the sea perfect for sailing and swimming. The third shell is a huge scallop shell. That makes sure all the beaches on Rainspell have sand and that all the rockpools are full of beautiful shells. If I could return all three shells to their cave then Jack Frost's palace would vanish and Rainspell would be back to normal again." She looked anxiously at the two girls. "Do...do you think you could help me?"

"Of course!" they both said.

Summer smiled. "Thank you!" Her smile faded. "Though I'm not sure how we can do it."

Kirsty looked at the castle. "We could fly closer and see if we can find any of the magic shells."

Rachel nodded. "But we'd better be careful of those goblins." Goblins were mean and horrible and would do anything to please Jack Frost.

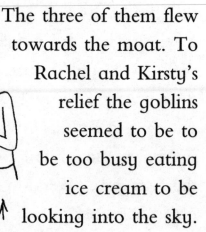

The three of them flew towards the moat. To Rachel and Kirsty's relief the goblins seemed to be to be too busy eating ice cream to be looking into the sky.

"Where have they got their ice creams from?" Kirsty whispered.

Summer sighed. "They've made it. Because they've got the shell that makes Rainspell holiday food taste yummy, they can make Rosie's special ice cream. Jack Frost is really pleased because it means that no one on the island can have Rosie's ice cream apart from him and his goblins."

One of the goblins – the one who was defending the drawbridge – didn't have an ice cream.

"Go on, give me some of yours," he grumbled to another goblin. "I can't leave the drawbridge or Jack Frost will be cross."

"Well, you're not having any of mine!" the goblin shouted back.

"Mmm, this is delicious!" another one teased the drawbridge goblin. "In fact, it's the best ice cream I ever tasted! Mmmm."

The drawbridge goblin stamped his foot. The other goblins walked off, laughing.

The goblin by the drawbridge was so angry that he hit the wall of the moat, almost knocking off a large twirly pink-and-cream shell.

"That goblin doesn't look very happy," Rachel commented.

Kirsty didn't reply. She was too busy staring at the drawbridge. "Look, Summer! The pink twisty shell," she breathed. "Is it one of the three magic shells?"

"Yes!" Summer exclaimed. "It is!"

Rachel looked at the big, scary goblin. "How are we going to get it back?"

"We could wait until the goblin
moves away," Kirsty suggested.

"We could be waiting for ages,"
Rachel pointed out.

"If only we could make the goblin
move," said Summer.

"Maybe he'll decide he can't wait for
an ice cream any longer," Rachel said
hopefully. "And he'll leave the
drawbridge."

"That's it!" Kirsty gasped. Rachel and

Summer looked at her. "You two could try and get the goblin to leave by telling him you've got some ice cream on the other side of that sand dune. Then I'll fly down and grab the magic shell."

"That's a brilliant idea!" Rachel said.

Summer nodded. "Come on! Let's go!"

The Magic Shell

Kirsty hovered in the air as Rachel and Summer flew towards the goblin.

"Oi!" he shouted as they swooped down. "What are you doing? Jack Frost said I shouldn't let any fairies into the palace!" He made a grab for Summer but she managed to dart out of his way.

"We're not trying to get into the castle,"

Rachel said, her heart pounding. The goblin looked even scarier close up. "We wanted to tell you that there's some ice cream on the other side of that sand dune."

The goblin frowned. "What sort of ice cream?"

"It's a special extra-delicious flavour that no one else here has tasted," Summer said.

The goblin looked interested. "Has it got chocolate sauce and sprinkles?"

"Oh yes," said Rachel. "Lots of sprinkles."

60

"I suppose I could just pop round to the other side of the sand dune," said the goblin. Then he shook his head. "I bet you fairies are trying to trick me. You just want to get into the castle." He flapped his hands at them. "Go away! Leave me alone!"

Summer and Rachel flew away in alarm.

"Didn't it work?" Kirsty asked, joining them.

"No," Rachel sighed. "He realised we were trying to trick him."

"Unless…" Summer said, her eyes lighting up, "…we make him believe we really do have an ice cream."

"But how can we do that?" said Rachel.

Summer grinned. "Like this!" She waved her wand. There was a loud splatting noise and two blobs of melted ice cream flew through the air. One landed on Rachel's T-shirt and another on Summer's pink sarong.

"Sorry!" Summer said, seeing Rachel's astonished face. "I know it's a bit sticky, but it might convince the goblin that we have some ice cream."

"I thought the goblins had all the ice cream magic?" said Kirsty, puzzled.

"They have the magic that makes the ice cream taste great," Summer explained. "I can still make ice cream, like Rosie can. It's just that it's all melted and sticky and wouldn't taste very nice." She looked at Rachel. "So what do you think?"

Rachel grinned. "I think it might just work!"

They flew down to the goblin again.

"I told you to go away!" he grumbled as they hovered just out of reach.

"I know. We tried to bring the ice cream to you, but it's too big to carry," said Rachel. "Look, it spilt all over our clothes."

The goblin peered at her T-shirt. "So there really is an ice cream over there?"

"Yes," Rachel replied. "But it's melting fast!"

The goblin jumped to his feet. "OK, show me where it is!"

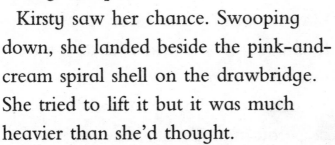

Rachel and Summer flew towards the sand dune. The goblin ran behind them, licking his lips.

Kirsty saw her chance. Swooping down, she landed beside the pink-and-cream spiral shell on the drawbridge. She tried to lift it but it was much heavier than she'd thought.

Come on, she thought frantically. She pulled harder.

"Quick, Kirsty!"

Kirsty looked around. Rachel and Summer were flying towards her at top speed. The goblin was chasing after them. He must have realised he'd been tricked when he didn't see any ice cream.

Kirsty gave the shell a last desperate tug. To her relief, it popped out of the sand. Flying upwards with it, she escaped from the goblin just in time.

"Hooray!" shouted Summer.

"You tricksy fairies!" shouted the goblin. "Come back here with that shell!"

Summer sped away with Kirsty and Rachel following her. As the girls flew over trees, the goblin's voice grew fainter.

"Jack Frost will be really angry when he hears what's happened, won't he?" Kirsty said.

Summer nodded. "We're going to have to watch out for him now he knows we're after the Rainspell Shells." She stroked the twirly curly shell. "At least we've got one of them back.

Come on, I'll show you the underwater cave."

Kirsty glanced at Rachel. "We ought to be getting back, really."

"Yes," Rachel agreed. "We told our parents we were only going for a short walk."

"Never mind," Summer replied. "You can always come and see the cave another time. After all, we've still got two more magic shells to find!" She flew up into the air. "See you soon!" Before she swooped away, she flicked her wand and the girls shot up to normal size again.

Rachel and Kirsty waved goodbye
and began the journey back to
the beach.

"That was fun!"
Rachel said.

As she spoke,
a shimmering haze
flickered through the
air and they heard
the faint sound of
ice cream bells.

"Something magic's
happening!" Kirsty exclaimed.

"Maybe Summer's putting the shell
back?" Rachel suggested.

They headed along the beach.

When they reached the road they
heard ice cream bells again. "More
magic?" Rachel said.

"No!" Kirsty cried. "Look!"

Rosie's ice cream van was driving along the road. "Hello, you two," Rosie called. "Great news! My ice cream machine is working again. In fact, the ice cream tastes even better than before!"

"That's fantastic!" Rachel said.

Rosie nodded. "I'm so happy, I've decided to give out free ice creams all afternoon. Would you like one?"

"Yes, please!" Rachel and Kirsty chorused.

Rachel chose a chocolate ice cream and Kirsty chose strawberry.

"Mmm, this really is delicious!" Rachel said. "Thanks, Rosie!"

"No problem," Rosie smiled and drove away.

Kirsty licked her cone. "It's brilliant Rosie's ice cream is back to normal, isn't it?"

Rachel nodded. "Yes, but we still need to do something about the sand and the seashells."

"We'll have to help Summer rescue the other Rainspell Shells," Kirsty said.

"We will," Rachel vowed. "We'll make Rainspell Island the perfect place for a holiday again. I just know we will!"

The Sea Breeze
Shell

Contents

What's Happened to the Wind?   77

The Goblin Regatta   87

Jack Frost   99

Sally's Tunnel   113

Escape!   129

What's Happened to the Wind?

"It's a wonderful day for the regatta, isn't it?" Kirsty said as she pulled on her trainers.

Rachel looked out of the window of Dolphin Cottage. There wasn't a cloud in the cornflower-blue sky. "It's perfect," she replied. "My dad's really excited."

Mr Walker and Mr Tate were hiring a boat to enter a race at the regatta.

Kirsty dropped her voice to a whisper. "At least Jack Frost won't be able to spoil today. It won't make a difference to the regatta that there aren't any shells or sand on the beach."

A shiver ran across Rachel's skin as

she thought about Jack Frost. She and Kirsty still had to help Summer the Holiday Fairy rescue the remaining two Rainspell shells. "Do you think we'll see Summer today?" she asked.

"I hope so!" Kirsty grinned.

The Walkers and the Tates walked to the harbour together.

"Goodness, it's hot," Mrs Walker said.

Mr Tate wiped his hand across his forehead. "I hope a breeze picks up. If there's no wind then the boats won't be able to sail."

"It's very strange," Kirsty's mum said. "It was so windy when we came over on the ferry!"

Rachel and Kirsty hurried ahead.
"Are you thinking
what I'm thinking?"
Kirsty hissed.

"That it could be
Jack Frost?" Rachel
whispered back.
"Maybe he is going to
spoil the regatta, after all!"

Their parents caught up with them.
"Let's try and stay together," Mrs
Walker said.

Crowds were thronging the pretty
streets that led down to the harbour.
Everyone looked hot and worried and
there was a long queue by Rosie's ice
cream van.

"There's the harbour master." Mr
Walker pointed to a man dressed in a

blue uniform. "He's in charge of the regatta. Let's find out what's going on."

The harbour master was talking to a group of people by the harbour clock.

"I'm very sorry," he was saying. "If the wind doesn't pick up in the next half hour, I'm afraid the regatta will be cancelled." There were groans from the crowd.

Kirsty and Rachel glanced at each other. They needed to talk!

"Can Kirsty and I go to the beach please?" Rachel asked.

"Yes, off you go," replied Mrs Walker. "Meet us by Rosie's van in half an hour.

If the race is going ahead we can watch it together."

"And if it isn't, we can all go home," said Mr Tate gloomily.

Rachel and Kirsty wriggled through the crowd and made their way on to the beach. They hurried across the pebbles until they were out of earshot of everyone else.

"We've got to do something!" Kirsty said. "I'm sure this is Jack Frost's fault. He's got the magic shell that controls the wind, hasn't he?"

Rachel nodded. "I bet he's trying to ruin everyone's day!" As she spoke, her foot knocked against a piece of driftwood. There was a merry tinkle and a fountain of golden sparks exploded into the air.

"Summer!" Rachel and Kirsty exclaimed as the holiday fairy flew out from under the driftwood and twirled into the sky.

"Hi there!" said Summer, smoothing down her pink sarong and grinning at them. "How are you?"

"Not great," Rachel admitted. "There's no wind so it looks like the regatta's going to be cancelled. Everyone's really upset."

Summer frowned. "Oh, it's all Jack Frost's fault! He's using the magic shell. He blew it this morning to get all the wind over to his side of the island for his regatta." She put her hands indignantly on her hips. "He is so mean!"

"Can we do anything to stop him?" asked Kirsty.

"The only way we can stop him is by getting that conch shell back," Summer replied. "Jack Frost's put it on one of the turrets on his castle. If we can rescue it then he won't be able to control the wind anymore."

Rachel and Kirsty exchanged determined looks. "Then let's go to the castle!" they said.

The Goblin Regatta

Summer waved her wand and a cloud
of golden dust floated over the girls.
Within seconds, they were fairies again.
They flew over the woods and the
tower until they arrived at Jack Frost's
sandcastle.

Loud yells and shouts were coming
from the direction of the beach.

"What's that noise?" Rachel wondered.

"I bet it's the goblins," Summer answered.

They swooped over the castle to investigate.

The goblins were sailing on the sea in a peculiar assortment of inflatable toys, with sails made out of beach towels and

picnic cloths. The makeshift boats bounced across the waves, only stopping when they hit another one. Half the goblins seemed to be in the water. The others were yelling rude things at each other. A tall goblin with a megaphone was standing on the beach shouting instructions, but everyone was ignoring him.

Kirsty looked back at the castle. It had three towers, a tall one in the middle and two shorter ones. The top of each tower was decorated with conch shells, shaped a bit like trumpets, creamy-brown on the outside and glossy pink inside.

"Which is the magic shell that controls the wind?" Kirsty asked.

"It's on the tower to the left." Summer pointed. "I think it's that shell with the brown stripes." She frowned. "Or maybe it's that one with the beige spots. No, no, I think it might be that large cream shell with no markings."

Rachel frowned. If Summer didn't know which shell it was, how could they possibly rescue it? "We have to know which shell it is," she said anxiously.

"Yes, Rachel's right," Kirsty put in.

"Don't worry," Summer smiled, glancing at the sky. "I think we'll find out any moment now!"

Just then, the sun suddenly came out from behind a cloud. As its rays fell on the towers, one of the shells began to glow. "Oh wow!" Kirsty breathed. "That has to be the magic shell!"

"It is," Summer said. "It always glitters in the sun. The question is, how are we going to rescue it? We can't just fly up and grab it because Jack Frost might see us." She pointed to a window near the top of the middle tower.

"He can't come outside because he'd
melt in the sun so he watches
everything from that window. He might
see us flying up to the tower!" She ran
a hand through her
blonde hair. "I think
the only way to get
the shell is by
getting into the
castle and going up
on the inside. Then we
can take the shell and sneak away."

"But what if Jack Frost notices that
the shell is missing before we get
away?" said Kirsty.

Rachel looked at the shells on the
beach and had an idea. "If we found
a shell that looked like the magic shell,
we could swap them over! Then Jack

Frost wouldn't know we'd taken it and we could escape before he realised."

"Oh yes!" Kirsty said.

Summer beamed. "Great idea! Come on!"

They flew down to the beach, keeping in the shadow of the castle walls. Luckily, none of the goblins noticed them – they were too busy squabbling.

"How are we going to get into the castle?" Kirsty wondered.

"Let's hide under this seaweed while we decide what to do," suggested Rachel. It was scary being on the beach with so many goblins around, especially when she was fairy-size. She lifted up a strand of seaweed.

"Hey!" a voice exclaimed. A large hermit crab without a shell was glaring at them from under the seaweed. "That was keeping me warm," he said, snapping his claws crossly.

Rachel and Kirsty backed away. "Oh, I'm sorry..." Rachel stammered.

"Henry!" cried Summer.

To Rachel and Kirsty's surprise, she hurried over and threw her arms around the crab. Smiling broadly, she turned to them. "Do you remember Henry? I had to build him a 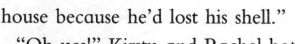 house because he'd lost his shell."

"Oh yes!" Kirsty and Rachel both exclaimed.

"Henry, this is Kirsty and Rachel," Summer said. "They're helping me to get the Rainspell Shells back. I'm sorry we moved your seaweed but we were trying to hide so the goblins didn't see us."

"Oh," Henry said, looking less cross.

"I'm sorry if I was a bit snappy just now, but I hate being without a shell. That's why I've come here. I thought I might find myself another one."

"There are loads of shells over here," said Rachel, turning round to tug at the seaweed. She broke off with a gasp of alarm. "Hide! Jack Frost is looking out of the tower!"

Jack Frost

A tall, bony figure was staring out of the window at the top of the tallest tower. His spiky hair stood out around his head and his beard was frozen into icicles. As he gazed around, the girls and Summer shrank back under the seaweed.

"Why aren't you having the race?" he shouted angrily to the goblins below.

Looking panicked, the goblin raised the megaphone. "Race, everyone!" he shouted. "Race!"

Immediately, all the goblins tried to sail in different directions. Four of the boats crashed into each other and two tipped right over.

Splash, went the goblins into the sea!

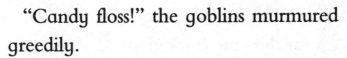

Grabbing a sun hat, Jack Frost shoved it on his head and leant out of the window. "Idiots! You couldn't entertain an icicle! Do something else. Play me some music instead. The goblin who plays me the best music will get to have as much candy floss as he can eat."

"Candy floss!" the goblins murmured greedily.

"The rest of you will get…" Jack Frost grinned nastily at the hopeful goblins, "…absolutely nothing!"

Laughing, he stomped back inside his tower.

The goblins on the beach scrabbled around, grabbing anything they could use for a musical instrument. They banged on upside-down buckets and blew shells as if they were horns. Rachel, Kirsty and Summer clapped their hands over their ears. The noise was deafening!

Rachel realised that this was their chance. The goblins were all so busy that the back door of the castle was unguarded. "Quick!" she hissed "Let's sneak in while they're not looking."

"We need to find a shell that looks like the magic shell first," Summer said.

"There's some over there." Kirsty pointed to where some goblins were arguing over a pile of conch shells.

A goblin with a big wart at the end of his nose was holding a beautiful cream shell.

"I want that one!" grumbled one of the other goblins.

"Well, you can't have it! It's mine!"

Clutching the shell, the warty-nosed goblin hurried away. He sat down on the sand near to the girls and Summer and started blowing into it. A couple of strangled toots came out.

The goblin shook the shell and tried again.

"That shell would be perfect," Kirsty breathed. "It looks just like the magic shell!"

"Yes," agreed Rachel, looking at the goblin. "But we need to persuade him to give it to us!"

Just then, Henry ambled out from under the seaweed. "That looks like it might be a good shell for me," he said, heading towards a yellow-and-white whelk shell. Then he shook his head.

"No," he sighed. "Its end is too pointy. Pointy shells are not comfortable homes. They're good for blowing through but not for living in."

Summer gasped. "Oh Henry, you've just given me an idea! Let's get the goblin to swap his conch shell for that pointy shell."

"How?" Kirsty asked.

Summer grinned. "With a little bit of magic, of course!"

She waved her wand, filling the air with golden sparkles and tiny glittering shells. As they fell on the whelk shell, the faint sound of a merry-go-round echoed through the air.

The goblin looked up. "What's that?"

"I've enchanted the shell so that it makes summery music," Summer whispered to Rachel and Kirsty.

Picking the shell up, she flew over to the goblin. "Excuse me!" she called.

Rachel and Kirsty joined her. Was this going to work?

The goblin frowned. "We're not supposed to let fairies anywhere near the castle. Be off with you!"

"But we've brought you a shell that plays brilliant music," Summer said.

"Music?" The goblin's eyes narrowed slyly. "Music that's good enough to win Jack Frost's competition?"

"Oh yes!" Kirsty said.

"Listen." Summer held up the shell. Merry-go-round music tinkled out.

"You'd easily win the competition with this shell," Rachel told him.

The goblin looked at them suspiciously. "My friend got into trouble when three pesky fairies tricked him and stole one of my master's shells. How do I know you're not playing a trick on me?"

"Us?" Rachel said, opening her eyes wide.

"We don't want to trick you," Kirsty said, trying to sound like she meant it. "We just want to help."

"You do want to win that competition, don't you?" added Summer. "Just think of the candy floss."

"Pink and sugary," Rachel added.

"Sticky and sweet..."

It was too much for the greedy goblin. "Give me that shell!" he shouted. Throwing the conch shell to the ground, he grabbed the pointy shell and blew hard. Lively music echoed through the air.

The goblin's face lit up. "I'm going to win the competition!" he cried. "I'm going to get all the candy floss!" He hurried back to the other goblins. "Listen, everyone!"

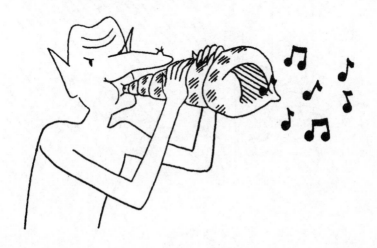

The girls and Summer watched as the other goblins crowded around him while the shell played its magic music.

"Come on!" Rachel urged Summer and Kirsty. "Let's go while they're busy!" She flew up into the air but then stopped. "Oh no!" she exclaimed. "Look at the doorway!"

The goblins were all pushing and

shoving as they fought to get into the castle to play their music to Jack Frost.

"We're never going to get in that way now!" Kirsty said in dismay.

Sally's Tunnel

"What are we going to do?"
Summer said, her face falling.

"You could always go a different
way," Henry said.

He scuttled towards the castle
walls and called, "Sally! Are you
there? I've got some friends who
need your help!"

Kirsty and Rachel stared in surprise as
a small browny-black
beetle suddenly
popped its head
out of the sand.
"Hello!" the
beetle said.

"Sally, these friends of mine are
trying to rescue a magic shell from the
tower," Henry explained.

"Pleased to meet you," Sally said.
"Follow me!" Swinging round, she
pushed her head against the castle wall
and began to burrow. Her legs moved
in a blur and sand flew up all around.
A few seconds later she was gone,
leaving a hole behind her.

"She's made a tunnel!"
Rachel gasped.

"Of course," beamed Summer. "Sand beetles love burrowing through sand. Come on! Don't forget the conch shell!"

Rachel and Kirsty helped her carry the shell over to the tunnel.

Summer stopped to kiss the hermit crab. "Goodbye Henry, see you soon."

"Bye, Henry," the girls called. "Good luck with finding a shell!"

It was a tight squeeze in the tunnel.
Rachel, Kirsty and Summer pushed the
shell upwards. The sandy walls were
rough against their knees and elbows.

"It's very dark," Kirsty puffed.

"I can fix that," Summer replied. She
waved her wand and a glow lit up the

dark, like the sun rising.

"Almost there!" Sally called out from up ahead. "We can't go all the way to the top of the tower because the sand is too soft. But I can take you to a staircase which will lead up to the turrets."

Rachel and Kirsty looked at each other nervously. What if they bumped into some goblins inside the castle, or, even worse, into Jack Frost himself?

A few minutes later, a circle of light appeared overhead.

"I'm out!" Sally called. "The coast is clear."

Rachel, Kirsty and Summer scrambled to the end of the tunnel and stepped cautiously into a narrow corridor.

Opposite them in the
sandy wall there was
an arched doorway
leading to some
stairs. Floating down
the stairs came the
sounds of goblins
blowing on shells
and Jack Frost's voice
snapping like broken ice.

"Useless! No! That won't do either!
No, that's useless too. Is that the best
you can do?"

Rachel shivered. "That staircase must
lead up to Jack Frost's room. Do you
think the goblin has shown him the
enchanted pointy shell yet?"

"It doesn't sound like it," said
Summer.

"If you don't mind, I'll be off," Sally
said. "I don't like goblins with
their big clumsy feet. My
aunt nearly got squashed
last week! Good luck!"
Waving a leg, she
burrowed back into the wall.

"Thanks, Sally!" the girls and Summer
called. They flew to the end of the
corridor and found the stairs that led to
the tower. They hurried up them until
they reached a big door at the top.
Pushing it open, they peeped out.

"We're here!" Summer exclaimed.

"And there's Jack Frost's window!" Rachel hissed, pointing to the next-door tower.

"Come on, let's swap the shells and get out of here," Kirsty said.

"But which is the magic shell?" Rachel asked.

They looked at the conch shells. The wind was blowing strongly and the sun was hidden behind the clouds. Without the sun, all the shells looked exactly the same!

"I know a way to tell, even when the sun isn't out," Summer said.

"All conch shells make a noise, apart
from the magic Rainspell shell. It
doesn't make a sound when it's blown;
it just makes the wind change. Let's get
blowing!"

The girls and Summer flew to the
first shell. Pushing their hair out of their
eyes, they began to blow down the
conches.

"Whoop!' went
the first one that
Kirsty choose.

"Toot!"
blew Rachel's.

"Whoa!" cried
Summer as a gust of
wind almost whisked her off
the tower. She grabbed at the nearest
conch shell to save herself and blew it.

It made a loud noise like a foghorn.

"Oh no!" Kirsty gasped, looking down. "The goblins in the boats are looking this way!"

She was right. The goblins who were still bobbing around in the sea were looking up. Some of them started to point and shout.

The girls and Summer flew frantically from shell to shell. They had to find the right one!

The goblins started to paddle towards the beach.

"We'll have to go!" Summer exclaimed.

Kirsty couldn't bear the thought of giving up when they were so close. She looked around desperately. Which was the magic shell?

"Come on, Kirsty!" cried Summer.

Kirsty suddenly had an idea. "I know! Why don't you use your wand like you did in the tunnel? The light that came from it then was just like sunlight. It might light up the magic shell!"

Summer stared at her. "You're right!" She waved her wand. There was a loud tinkling sound and the wand lit up with a golden glow. Summer swept the wand through the air and the glow moved like a torch-beam through the grey air. As the light fell on the shells, one a few metres away from Kirsty began to sparkle.

"The magic conch shell!" Kirsty gasped, running over. She blew into it just to make sure.

The shell didn't make a sound.

"Rachel!" Kirsty cried. "We've found the shell!"

"I know!" Rachel replied. "Look at the goblins!"

Kirsty looked round. The magic shell had made the wind on the beach whip into a gale. The goblins started yelling as their boats were tossed about.

"Did I just do that?" Kirsty said.

Summer nodded. "Quick! Let's swap the shells over!"

Rachel pulled the magic shell out of the wall and Kirsty stuck the new shell in its place. Hearts racing, they hurried back to the door and raced down the stairs. As they flew into the empty corridor they could see the hole in the wall where Sally's tunnel started.

Suddenly Summer stopped dead, and the girls nearly crashed into her.

The goblin with the warty nose had come running into the corridor. Carrying the pointy shell under one arm, he charged straight towards them!

Escape!

Rachel and Kirsty froze.

"I've got the best shell and I'm going to have all the candy floss!" the goblin muttered, running towards them.

Summer gasped. "He hasn't seen us!" Grabbing Rachel and Kirsty's arms, she pulled them up to the ceiling.

Licking his lips, the goblin charged through the door that led to Jack Frost's tower. The shell's music seemed to be slowing down, getting fainter with every second, just like a real merry-go-round when it comes to a stop.

"The magic's about to wear out!" Summer exclaimed. "Come on, let's get out of here before Jack Frost realises he's been tricked!" She dived into the tunnel.

"If we slide down, it'll be quicker," Summer said.

She touched the sand at the bottom of the tunnel with her wand. The surface began to glitter like glass. With a loud "Whee!" Summer whizzed off down the tunnel as if it was a giant slide.

Kirsty and Rachel flung themselves down behind her. Sandy walls flashed by as they hurtled down the twisting tunnel and fairy dust sparkled around them.

Clutching the magic shell, Rachel shot
out on to the pile of
seaweed at the bottom.
Kirsty almost landed
on top of her.

"Wow! That
was brilliant!"
Rachel gasped,
scrambling to her feet.

Suddenly above them there was a yell
so loud that it made the castle walls
shake. "WHAT? You're telling me you
got this useless shell from three fairies?"

Although Jack Frost was in his tower,
the girls could hear him as clearly as if
he was standing next to them. "Well it
doesn't make music now!" he shouted.
There was a pause. "What do you
mean, you swapped it for a conch shell?

A conch shell!"

"Quick!" Summer looked alarmed.
"I think Jack Frost has just realised we
tricked the goblin!"

As they flew up into the air, they saw
Jack Frost storm to the window. "Pesky
fairies!" he shouted. "Come back here
with my magic shell!"

But he was too far away to stop
them. With a final look at the castle,
the girls and Summer raced away.

"Phew!" Rachel said as they reached the harbour. "That was scary!"

"Yes," Summer agreed. "But at least we rescued the magic shell! Do you want to come to the underwater cave and help me put it back where it belongs?"

Kirsty looked at the boats bobbing on the calm sea. "We should get back to the regatta. We said we'd meet our mums to watch the race."

"Although it doesn't look like there's going to be a race," Rachel sighed. "There's still not enough wind for the boats to sail."

"But as soon as I put the shell back, the wind will return," Summer reminded her.

Kirsty glanced at the big clock on the

harbour wall. Almost half
an hour had passed
since they had left
their dads with the
harbour master.
"I don't think that's
going to be quick enough.
The harbour master must be about
to make a decision any moment now,"
she said, feeling very disappointed.

"You mean, you need wind right
now?" Summer asked.

Rachel and Kirsty nodded.

"No problem!" Summer exclaimed.
She swooped down to a rock and raised
the shell to her lips. At once a breeze
swirled across the beach.

"The shell's bringing the wind back!"
Kirsty exclaimed.

Summer grinned and blew harder. With every breath, the wind grew stronger until the sails of the boats were flapping in the breeze.

Lowering the shell, Summer smiled at Rachel and Kirsty. "I think your dads will be able to race now." She waved her wand and a cloud of sparkling dust floated around them.

Kirsty and Rachel shot back to their normal size.

"Thanks, Summer!" they grinned.

"Thank you," said the fairy. "See you soon!"

In the distance there was a loud hooting noise. "The race is about to start!" Kirsty exclaimed. "Come on, Rachel!"

Waving goodbye to Summer the two girls ran across the pebbles.

As they reached the ice cream van they heard the horn sound again. The breeze swelled the sails, and the boats shot across the starting line.

"Come on, Dad!" Rachel and Kirsty shouted as their dads' boat raced towards the finishing line. Their boat, the Merry Sue, was just in front of the others!

"They've won!" cheered Mrs Tate.

Rachel beamed at Kirsty. "I'm very glad we got the shell back."

"Me too," Kirsty agreed. "And now there's just one more shell to rescue."

Rachel grinned at her. "We'll get it back. I know we will!"

The Magic
Scallop Shell

Contents

No Donkey Rides!   145

Summer Magic   151

Trapped!   159

Escape!   171

The Underwater Cave   179

No Donkey Rides!

The sun was shining and a breeze was blowing white cotton-wool clouds across the sky as Rachel and Kirsty ran down to the beach. It was a perfect day for donkey riding!

"It's very quiet," said Kirsty. Usually there were lots of people, playing, swimming and sunbathing, but ever since Jack Frost had magicked the sand and shells to his castle, people had stayed away from the beach.

Rachel nodded. "It just isn't the same without the sand. We have to get the last Rainspell shell back." She spotted Mr Williams and his four fluffy donkeys. Mr Williams was holding up the smallest donkey's leg and checking its hoof. "At least the donkeys are still here," Rachel added.

She and Kirsty headed over.

"Hello, Mr Williams," Kirsty called. "Can we have a ride please?"

Mr Williams shook his head. "I'm afraid not. The beach is too rocky. Pippin has hurt her hoof from treading on a stone."

"Oh, no!" Kirsty stroked the donkey's velvety nose. "Will she be OK?"

"She'll be fine after a day's rest," Mr Williams replied. "But there won't be any more donkey rides while the beach is like this." He sighed. "I'd better take them back to their field."

Rachel and Kirsty watched as Mr Williams led the unhappy donkeys away.

"Jack Frost is determined to spoil everyone's holiday, isn't he?" Rachel said sadly.

Suddenly Kirsty pointed to a rockpool. "Look! I saw some sparkles over there."

A cloud of golden dust whooshed up from behind a rock and the Holiday Fairy spiralled into the air. "Hello!"

Summer landed on Kirsty's shoulder, light as a feather. "I've found out where Jack Frost's keeping the magic scallop shell!" she exclaimed. "He's using it to decorate his throne in the Great Hall." Summer clasped her hands together. "It's going to be very tricky to rescue the shell, the trickiest one of all! But if we don't put it back in its underwater cave, the beaches on Rainspell will stay sandless forever!"

"We can't let that happen!" said Rachel.

Kirsty nodded. "It might be dangerous, but we're not going to give up!"

Summer waved her wand, showering Rachel and Kirsty with fairy dust. At once they shrank to fairy-size.

"It's not going to be easy to get in this time," Summer warned as they flew over the island. "Jack Frost is so angry about losing the other two shells that he's put extra goblins on guard duty."

Sure enough, when they reached the castle, there were goblins everywhere – on the drawbridge and by the door, walking around the towers and patrolling the beach.

Kirsty noticed that the windows in the castle looked rather unusual. She flew to a nearby window and touched the glass. It was freezing cold! "It's made of ice!" she gasped.

"All the windows are," Summer replied. "Jack Frost has put a spell on them so they won't melt in the sun, but my special summer magic can make a hole just big enough for us to get through." She looked anxiously at the goblins below. "Shall we fly to the back of the castle where it's quieter?"

Rachel and Kirsty nodded and they all flew around to the other side of the castle. They stopped beside a small window near the bottom of a tower.

"Here goes," Summer grinned. Her wand glowed brightly as she touched it against the icy window.

There was a fizzing sound and the
ice began to melt around
tip of the wand.

"It's working!"
Kirsty whispered.

"Keep going,
Summer. It's almost
big enough for us to
get through!" urged
Rachel. Concentrating
hard, Summer made a perfectly round
hole in the window. "Phew!' she said.

She looked pale under her freckles.

"Are you OK?" Rachel asked.

Summer nodded. "Just tired. Jack
Frost's spell is strong and melting the
ice is very difficult." She waved her
wand. Usually a cloud of glittering
fairy dust whooshed out, but now only

a few sparkles floated into the sky.
"There's not much magic left in my
wand," she said, looking worried. She
began to squeeze through the hole.

"Come on. Let's go
and rescue the last
Rainspell shell!"

Rachel and
Kirsty followed
her through the
window. It led into
a narrow corridor.

"Be careful!" Summer whispered.
"The Great Hall is this way."

They flew cautiously along the
corridor, staying near the ceiling
where the shadows were darkest. Rachel
could feel her skin prickling. What if
a goblin came along the corridor?

Or, even worse, what if Jack Frost did?

There were large footprints in the sand on the floor.

"Goblin footprints," Summer whispered nervously.

They flew down a set of stairs and along another corridor until they came to a big wooden door.

"This is the door to the Great Hall," Summer told the girls.

Rachel pushed the door open a little way and peeped in. "There's no one here," she said in relief. A magnificent throne stood in the middle of the empty room. Icicles hung off its arms and its back was carved out of ice in the shape of a large scallop shell. A real scallop shell was stuck to the very top. Its wavy white edge glowed with golden fairy dust.

"It's the magic shell," Summer breathed.

"Quick!" Kirsty said. "Let's get it before anyone comes!"

The three of them flew over and took hold of the shell. It came loose with the faintest sound of tinkling fairy music.

"Stop right there!" A cold voice snapped through the air.

Rachel, Kirsty and Summer spun around.

Jack Frost was standing in the doorway!

Trapped!

"Quick!" Rachel gasped. "We've got to do something!"

Jack Frost raised his hands but Summer was quicker. Waving her wand so that it flared like a candle, she pointed it at the sandy floor. There was a sizzling sound and the floor glowed red-hot.

With a cry, Jack Frost leapt back.
"Ow! The floor's hot." The icicles on
his beard began to drip.

"Melt the window, Summer!" Kirsty
cried. "Let the sunshine in!"

Summer raced to the window and
touched the pane with her wand. There
was a faint fizzing noise and a very
small patch on the window started to
melt. "My wand's running out
of magic!" Summer gasped.

"Freeze!" Jack Frost ordered, pointing
his fingers at the floor.

Rachel watched in dismay as the red
glow faded from the
floor. "Quick,
Summer!" she urged.

"Come on,
wand!" Summer
whispered. There
was a sizzle and then
a loud snap as a maze
of splinters spread across the ice.

Crack! The window shattered!
Sunlight came streaming in.

Jack Frost stumbled backwards with
his hands over his eyes. "Guards!" he
shouted.

"Let's go!" Kirsty said, flying into the
air with Rachel. "Come on, Summer!"

But Summer didn't move. She
lay on the window ledge, panting.

Her face was white and her wand had lost all its sparkle.

Kirsty and Rachel swooped down and

tried to help Summer up. "Can't move…" Summer murmured. "Too tired…no magic left…"

"Don't worry," Rachel said, trying to stay calm although her heart was thudding. "We'll help you. Kirsty, can you take the shell while I carry Summer?"

Kirsty nodded. Rachel put her arms around the little fairy and flew upwards, straining hard. Even though the fairy was tiny, it was very difficult

to fly with her. Summer hung limply,
her wings drooping and her eyes closed.

"Guards!" Jack Frost yelled again.

"Quick, Rachel, through the
window!" said Kirsty.

Jack Frost raised his hands and a gust
of freezing air filled the room. With a
loud crackle, the window froze over
with a fresh sheet of glittering ice.

Kirsty looked round desperately. There was a narrow staircase on the other side of the room. "Let's go that way!" she called to Rachel.

Carrying Summer and the shell, the two girls flew across the room and up the spiral staircase. Below, there was the sound of pounding feet and shouting. The goblins!

"Stop those fairies NOW!" Jack Frost yelled, and the goblins started to run up the stairs.

Kirsty spotted a window ahead. "If only Summer's wand hadn't used up all its magic, we could

have melted our way out," she panted.
Just then, the two girls heard a faint
scratching noise and a little voice
singing, "All day long, I dig
and dig. All day long
I dig and dig…"
"I know that voice!"
Rachel gasped. "It's
Sally the sand-beetle!"
A little browny-
black beetle popped
her head out of the
wall. "Hello again!"
Sally said in surprise.
"What are you doing
here?" She looked
at Summer and her eyes
stretched wide. "What's happened?"
"It's a long story," Kirsty replied.

"We really need to get out of here, Sally!" Rachel said. "And fast!"

"Come here, you pesky fairies!" the goblins shouted as they charged up the staircase.

"Quick!" said Sally. "Follow me!"

Her legs whirred as she made the tunnel bigger. Kirsty dived in, hugging the shell in her arms. Rachel pulled Summer in after her. They only just made it before the goblins rushed around the corner. The girls held their breath and kept very still.

Would the goblins notice the tunnel?

To their relief, the heavy footsteps thudded past and carried on up the stairs.

Kirsty and Rachel slithered through the tunnel with Summer and the magic shell. It led to a narrow window ledge on the other side of the castle wall.

"That was close!" Sally said, waving her feelers.

"Very," Kirsty agreed.

"We can't stay here," Rachel said, glancing at the window behind them. "The goblins might see us."

"Can't you fly away?" Sally asked.

Kirsty shook her head, trying not to look down. The beach was a long way below them! "There's no way we could carry Summer and the shell."

"Oh, what are we going to do?" Rachel said desperately.

"Caw!"

They all jumped and looked up.
A black-headed seagull was flying
towards them.

"Do you fairies need some help?"
he called.

Escape!

The seagull looked as huge as a horse, but his black eyes were kind and anxious.

"My name's Gregory," he cawed. "Is there something wrong with Summer?"

"She's used up all her magic against Jack Frost," Rachel explained.

Summer groaned and her eyelids flickered.

"We need to take the magic scallop shell back to the underwater cave," said Kirsty.

"No problem," Gregory declared. "Climb on to my back and I'll fly you down to the sea."

The girls didn't need telling twice. Rachel scrambled on first with Summer, and Kirsty followed with the scallop shell. Digging their hands into the soft

white feathers on Gregory's back, they held on tight.

At that moment, the goblins ran down the stairs. Gregory flapped his powerful wings and flew away from the window ledge. The goblins ran to the window and pointed but they were too late!

"We're safe!" Rachel shouted as the wind swept through her hair.

"NO!" They turned and saw Jack Frost standing at the window of the Great Hall. "You pesky fairies!" he yelled. "Bring back that shell!"

"Never!" Kirsty shouted back and she laughed in glee as Gregory swooped over the sea.

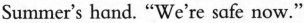

"Oh goodness," Summer mumbled, starting to wake up. "I don't feel very well. Everything's swaying."

"It's OK. We're on Gregory's back," Rachel told her. She squeezed Summer's hand. "We're safe now."

"I'm afraid I can only take you as far as the surface of the sea," Gregory called over his shoulder. "You'll need to swim the rest of the way to the cave."

Kirsty looked worriedly at Rachel. "How are we going to do that? We can't breathe underwater."

"Don't worry," said Summer, trying to sit up. "We can use fairy magic."

"But your wand has run out of magic," Rachel reminded her.

"We don't need my wand," Summer replied. She was looking much better now. "What we need is this!" She rummaged in her beach bag and pulled out a sparkling pink bottle.

"It's a bottle of bubble mixture!" Kirsty said, as Summer pulled out a small bubble wand with a circle at one end.

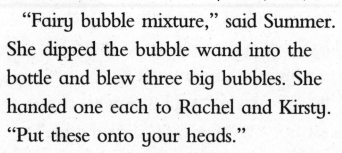

"Fairy bubble mixture," said Summer. She dipped the bubble wand into the bottle and blew three big bubbles. She handed one each to Rachel and Kirsty. "Put these onto your heads."

The bubbles sank down over their faces until their heads were completely enclosed. They looked just like old-fashioned divers' helmets!

Summer patted the seagull's smooth feathers. "Goodbye, 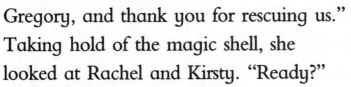 Gregory, and thank you for rescuing us." Taking hold of the magic shell, she looked at Rachel and Kirsty. "Ready?"

They nodded nervously. The sea beneath them looked very deep!

"One, two, three...JUMP!" Summer cried.

The Underwater Cave

Down, down, down, Rachel and Kirsty
went into the deep water. At first they
both held their breath, but they soon
realised they didn't need to. With the
fairy helmets on, they could breathe
underwater! Fairy magic also seemed
to be keeping them warm because the
water didn't feel cold at all.

"Wow!" Kirsty said, gazing around. The seabed was covered with beautiful pink, peach and white coral. Anemones waved their tentacles and shoals of brightly coloured fish swept by.

"It's beautiful!" Rachel gasped.

Summer bobbed beside her, grinning. "Let's go to the cave." She gave a whistle and three beautiful golden seahorses came swimming up. Bubbles trailed from their flared nostrils.

"They're wearing bridles!" Rachel exclaimed.

"Jump on!" said Summer. With one arm clutching the magic shell, she mounted the first seahorse.

The other two seahorses bobbed over to Rachel and Kirsty. The girls scrambled onto their backs and the seahorses set off. They whooshed through the water, dodging past seaweed and swerving around shoals of fish. Rachel and Kirsty laughed out. It was the most exciting ride ever!

"Here's the cave!" Summer called at last.

A small underwater cave appeared
ahead, hollowed out of the rocks. The
surface of the sea was far above,
glittering in the sun. Getting
off the seahorses, Rachel,
Kirsty and Summer
swam into the cave.

The floor was
covered with tiny pink
shells. Three stone
shelves were spaced
around the walls.
On one shelf was the
glittering twisty, curly
shell they had rescued
from the drawbridge. On
the next shelf was the glowing cream
conch shell they had taken from the
tower. The third shelf was empty.

"That's where this shell belongs,"
Summer explained. She carefully propped
the white scallop shell onto the shelf.

At once a fountain of pink and golden
sparkles fizzed into the water. The girls
heard a low rumbling noise. It got louder
and louder, filling the cave. It ended with
a loud crash, and then there was silence.

"What was that?' Kirsty breathed,
taking her hands away from her ears.

Summer stared at her with huge eyes.
"I think that was Jack Frost's castle
falling down."

"Look at your wand, Summer!"
Rachel gasped. The fairy's wand was
glittering gold again and sparkles trailed
from the tip.

"My wand has filled up with fairy
magic!" Summer cried in delight.

They swam back to the seahorses
and rode up to the surface of the sea.

"The castle's gone!" said Kirsty, staring at
the cove where Jack Frost's castle had been.

There was nothing left at all, just
a thick layer of soft yellow sand on
the beach.

Summer, Rachel and Kirsty said goodbye
to the seahorses and, shaking their wings
dry, flew into the air. The bubbles popped
on their heads as they soared up.

"Look! Someone's written in the sand!"

Rachel pointed to the beach where the castle had been.

Large spiky letters spelled out: YOU CAN'T CATCH ME!

"It looks like Jack Frost got away," said Kirsty.

Summer nodded. "But that doesn't matter. The important thing is whether Rainspell's got its holiday magic back. Let's go and see!"

They flew to the other side of the island.

"Look!" Rachel gasped. Golden sand stretched from the white cliffs down to the blue sea. Rockpools glittered in the sun, and the beach was dotted with shells in every colour of the rainbow.

Children laughed and shouted as they ran across the sand with buckets and spades. By the harbour, Rosie's ice cream van tinkled a merry tune, and Mr Williams was leading his donkeys back down to the beach.

"Thank you so much for helping me get Rainspell's holiday magic back," Summer said, giving Kirsty and Rachel a hug.

"That's OK," Rachel smiled.

"I'm just glad we could help," Kirsty added. "It's been really fun." She looked down. "There are our mums and dads!"

The Walkers and the Tates were heading down the path with towels, beach bags and a picnic hamper.

The girls and Summer flew down to the beach. Summer waved her wand and the girls shot back to their normal size.

"Bye, Summer," Kirsty said. "I'll miss you, and your summer magic."

Summer grinned. "Don't worry, you haven't seen the last of it yet." She twirled around. "Bye!" she called, darting away in a cloud of golden sparkles.

"Hi, girls!" Mr Walker called as they ran over a few minutes later. "Isn't it great? A freak wind blew all the sand back on to the beach again.

It was like magic!"

Rachel and Kirsty grinned at each other.

"Let's have our picnic over here," Mrs Tate said, starting to unpack. There were sandwiches, cold sausages, bags of crisps, bottles of Coca Cola and tubs of juicy red strawberries.

"This looks delicious," Kirsty said, helping to put out some plates.

"I'd like to have a swim before lunch," Rachel said.

"Me too!" Kirsty agreed.

"Well, we've brought your beach bags with us," Mrs Walker said. "Why don't you get changed?"

They nodded and took their beach bags behind a large rock.

"Oh!" Rachel gasped as she opened her bag. "Look!" She pulled out a gorgeous swimsuit. It had lilac and pink stripes, and it shimmered with silver glitter.

Kirsty looked in her bag. "I've got one too! They must be a magic present from Summer to say thank you!"

"I'm so glad Rainspell's back to normal," Rachel said as they changed into their new swimsuits. "This is going to be the best holiday ever now!"

"It really is," Kirsty agreed.

Shouting and laughing, the two girls raced across the sand, which seemed softer and more golden than ever before, and splashed into the sparkling sea.

Win a Rainbow Magic
Sparkly T-Shirt and Goody Bag!

There are seven magic shells in *Summer the Holiday Fairy* and each one has a secret letter in it. Find all seven letters and re-arrange them to make a special Fairyland word, then send it to us. Each month we will put the entries into a draw and select one winner to receive a Rainbow Magic Sparkly T-shirt and Goody Bag!

Send your entry on a postcard to Rainbow Magic Holiday Competition, Orchard Books, 96 Leonard Street, London EC2A 4XD. Australian readers should write to Hodder Headline Australia, Level 17/207 Kent Street, Sydney, NSW 2000. Don't forget to include your name and address. Only one entry per child. Final draw: 28th April 2006.

Good luck!

Have you checked out the

Website at:

www.rainbowmagic.co.uk

There are games, activities and fun things to do, as well as news and information about Rainbow Magic and all of the fairies.

RAINBOW magic

by Daisy Meadows

Ruby the Red Fairy	ISBN	1 84362 016 2
Amber the Orange Fairy	ISBN	1 84362 017 0
Saffron the Yellow Fairy	ISBN	1 84362 018 9
Fern the Green Fairy	ISBN	1 84362 019 7
Sky the Blue Fairy	ISBN	1 84362 020 0
Izzy the Indigo Fairy	ISBN	1 84362 021 9
Heather the Violet Fairy	ISBN	1 84362 022 7

The Weather Fairies

Crystal the Snow Fairy	ISBN	1 84362 633 0
Abigail the Breeze Fairy	ISBN	1 84362 634 9
Pearl the Cloud Fairy	ISBN	1 84362 635 7
Goldie the Sunshine Fairy	ISBN	1 84362 641 1
Evie the Mist Fairy	ISBN	1 84362 636 5
Storm the Lightning Fairy	ISBN	1 84362 637 3
Hayley the Rain Fairy	ISBN	1 84362 638 1

The Party Fairies

Cherry the Cake Fairy	ISBN	1 84362 818 X
Melodie the Music Fairy	ISBN	1 84362 819 8
Grace the Glitter Fairy	ISBN	1 84362 820 1
Honey the Sweet Fairy	ISBN	1 84362 821 X
Polly the Party Fun Fairy	ISBN	1 84362 822 8
Phoebe the Fashion Fairy	ISBN	1 84362 823 6
Jasmine the Present Fairy	ISBN	1 84362 824 4
Holly the Christmas Fairy	ISBN	1 84362 661 6

All priced at £3.99. Holly the Christmas Fairy priced at £4.99.
Rainbow Magic books are available from all good bookshops, or can be ordered
direct from the publisher: Orchard Books, PO BOX 29, Douglas IM99 1BQ
Credit card orders please telephone 01624 836000
or fax 01624 837033 or visit our Internet site: www.wattspub.co.uk
or e-mail: bookshop@enterprise.net for details.

To order please quote title, author and ISBN and your full name and address.
Cheques and postal orders should be made payable to 'Bookpost plc.'
Postage and packing is FREE within the UK
(overseas customers should add £2.00 per book).
Prices and availability are subject to change.